DATE DUE

APR 21 '93	OCT 29 '94	MAY 0 4 2002
MAY 24 '93	MAR 18 '95	JAN. 2 5 2003
JUL 10 '93	JUL 15 '96	JUL 0 1 2003
AUG 14 '93	JUL 24 '96	JUN. 1 5 2004
AUG 17 '93	OCT 2 9 1997	NOV. 0 2 2005
NOV 17 '93	DEC - 6 1997	JUL 1 6 2009
JUL 2- '94	FEB 1 8 1998	DEC 1 1 2009
JUL 16 '94	MAY 1 1 1998	SEP - 2 2013
AUG 8- '94	JUL 2 9 1998	AUG - 4 2014
SEP 5- '94	APR 2 6 1999	AUG 0 1 2016
SEP 24 '94	APR 2 4 2000	
OCT 1- '94	OCT 3 1 2000	

F
Sin   Singer, A. L.
        Disney's Aladdin

Disney's Aladdin

Disney's Aladdin

Adapted from the film by
A. L. Singer

DISNEY PRESS

NEW YORK

First Edition
1   3   5   7   9   10   8   6   4   2

Library of Congress Catalog Card Number: 91-58972
ISBN 1-56282-241-1

15909

In a faraway land, where the sun scorches the fiery desert, there lies an ancient secret.

It is a lamp, long forgotten and buried deep beneath the shifting sands. It is small and simple. It bears no fancy design and contains no precious jewels. To all but the wisest among us, it would appear dull and worthless.

But this lamp is not what it seems. Long ago, it held the greatest power in all the lands of Arabia. Its magic changed forever the course of a young man's life. A young man who, like the lamp, was more than what he seemed.

The tale begins on a dark night, where a dark man waits with a dark purpose. . . .

CHAPTER ONE

*T*he man's name was Jafar, and he was prepared to wait. His beady eyes and pointed turban gave him the look of a cobra about to strike. Perched on his shoulder, a parrot cocked its head impatiently. Beneath him, his horse shifted and gave a restless snort.

The treasure was buried out there somewhere. Only one person would be able to find it—the person who possessed two halves of an ancient scarab. Jafar had one half, and soon he would have the other. Then the treasure would be his. And with it, he would become the most powerful man in Agrabah.

In the stillness, Jafar heard the clopping of hooves as a rider approached.

The man was a common thief named Gazeem, and he had agreed to bring Jafar the other half of the scarab—in return for a part of the treasure. Jafar had promised.

Jafar had lied.

"You are late," he said.

Gazeem dismounted and bowed his head. Jafar was

the royal vizier, the chief adviser to the sultan. It was not wise to upset him. "My apologies, O Patient One," Gazeem said.

Jafar glared. "You have it, then?"

With a grin, the thief pulled half the scarab from his pocket.

Jafar reached for it, but the thief held it back. "What about the treasure? You promised me. . . ."

Screech! The parrot swooped down from Jafar's shoulder, grabbed the scarab, and dropped it into Jafar's bony hand.

"Trust me," Jafar said. "You'll get what's coming to you."

Quickly he took out his half of the scarab. He could feel his blood pounding as he fit the halves together. They glowed. Then . . .

BOOOOOM! A clap of thunder shook the desert. The scarab leapt from Jafar's hand as if it were alive. It streaked across the dunes in a blaze of light.

Jafar spurred on his horse. "Quickly, follow the trail!" he shouted.

Gazeem mounted his own horse and raced after Jafar. Bright as a comet, the scarab shot toward a small sandstone. It circled around it, then paused in the air.

Crack! The scarab suddenly split into halves again and plunged into the rock, each half wedging into a small hole.

Jafar stopped his horse and jumped off. The pulsing scarab stared out at him like a huge pair of eyes. An exhilarating chill bolted through him. There was no turning back now.

RRRRRRROMMMMMM! The earth began to tremble. The strange eyes flashed wildly. Gazeem cowered in fright.

Slowly the rock began to grow upward. It expanded in all directions, changing shape. The eyes remained, and now ears formed, then a nose. Last was a mouth, huge and gaping. A column of white light burst from within, almost blinding Jafar.

The rock was now a tiger face, frozen in a furious, silent roar. Jafar stared in awe. His frightened parrot clung to his shoulder, digging in its claws.

"By Allah!" Gazeem murmured. "A tiger-god!"

"At last, Iago!" Jafar said to his parrot. "After all my years of searching—the Cave of Wonders!"

"*Awk!*" Iago screeched. "Cave of Wonders!"

Jafar pulled Gazeem close to him. "Now, remember," he snarled. "Bring me the lamp. The rest of the treasure is yours, but the *lamp* is *mine!*"

Gazeem swallowed hard. He turned toward the mouth of the tiger-god and began walking slowly.

"*Awk!* The lamp!" Iago repeated, loud enough for Gazeem to hear. Then he leaned in close to Jafar's ear and whispered, "Geez, where'd you dig this bozo up?"

"Ssshh!" Jafar snapped. Iago allowed no one to know he could speak like a human—no one except his master, that is. But right now, Jafar was in no mood to listen. He was watching. Watching and waiting.

"*Who disturbs my slumber?*" boomed the tiger-god, its voice rumbling the ground once again.

"Er . . . it is I, Gazeem, a humble thief." His voice was a nervous squeak, and his knees felt weak and shaky.

"*Know this!*" the tiger-god said. "*Only one may enter here. One whose rags hide a heart that is pure— the Diamond in the Rough!*"

Gazeem cast a doubtful glance behind him. "Go on!" Jafar commanded.

Frightened, Gazeem turned back toward the cave's opening. A flight of stairs led downward into . . . what? He couldn't tell. Carefully he began walking down.

4

RRRRRAAAAUUUGGHHHHH! The tiger-god's thunderous roar was like nothing Jafar had ever heard. Gazeem's shriek could be heard only for a moment, and then the tiger-god's mouth slammed shut, silencing the thief forever.

"Seek thee out the Diamond in the Rough!" the tiger-god commanded.

Slowly the rock collapsed into a mound of sand. The scarab halves flickered, then went dark.

Jafar stared in silence as Iago dove into the mound and resurfaced, spitting out sand. He picked the scarab halves up and flew back to Jafar. "I can't believe this!" Iago said. "We're never going to get ahold of that stupid lamp!"

"Patience, Iago, patience. Gazeem was obviously less than worthy."

"Now *there's* a big surprise!" Iago said, rolling his eyes. "So what are we going to do! We've got a big problem here—"

But Jafar just reached out and squeezed Iago's beak shut. He needed quiet. "Only one may enter . . . ," he said. "I must find this one—this Diamond in the Rough."

The Diamond in the Rough—Jafar understood what

5

that meant. A common person, poor and unwashed, who had shining qualities within.

There was only one way to seek this person out, and Jafar knew just how to do it.

An evil grin spread across his face. He hadn't gotten the treasure tonight, but no matter.

He was close—oh so close. And before long, his waiting would be over.

CHAPTER TWO

S top, thief!"

The guard shouted at the top of his lungs as he chased a raggedly dressed boy through the crowded marketplace of Agrabah.

The boy zigzagged skillfully around the outdoor stands—fruit sellers, clothing merchants, bakers, trinket sellers. In his right hand, he clutched a loaf of bread. Beside him ran a small monkey dressed in a vest and a hat.

"I'll get you, street rat!" the guard shouted.

Street rat. If there was one name Aladdin hated, that was it. The sultan's guards looked down on the poor people of Agrabah—people such as himself. Sure, he swiped food sometimes. He had no choice—he had to eat. But he was no street rat.

"Come on, Abu!" Aladdin called to his pet monkey. He ran to a nearby house and leapt onto its low, flat roof. Then he and Abu sprinted from rooftop to rooftop, landing on a pair of clotheslines and finally falling into a soft pile of clothes.

Instantly he was snatched up by a pair of thick, hairy hands.

It was Rasoul, the head of the sultan's guard. Rasoul was a man of few words, but if there was one thing he did well, it was catching young thieves.

"Gotcha!" Rasoul said, lifting Aladdin up.

Abu leapt onto Rasoul's shoulder and shoved the guard's turban over his eyes. Aladdin quickly wrenched himself free, and he and Abu bolted away. They wove through the marketplace, past a camel salesman, a rug merchant, a jewelry cart. . . .

Suddenly Abu stopped. The little monkey's eyes were fixed on the cart. Abu had one big weakness—sparkling jewels. He crouched beside the cart, reaching up to steal a pendant.

"Stop him!" someone yelled. Dozens of faces turned toward Abu.

Aladdin spun around. He grabbed Abu by the back of his neck. To their right, the guards charged closer. To their left, angry townspeople closed in. Aladdin and Abu ran straight ahead toward a stairway that led to a tall tower. They raced up the stairs and in through a window. Aladdin grabbed a rug, and using it as a parachute, he and Abu leapt from another window to the other side of the building. They jumped again, this time landing safely in a quiet little alley, darkened by the shadow of the sultan's palace doors.

There the sounds of the marketplace were muffled. Aladdin exhaled and sat down. He was *starving*.

"All right, Abu, now we feast!" he said, breaking the loaf of bread in half.

But before he could eat, he saw a frail boy and girl in the shadows. They said nothing, but their wide, staring eyes spoke for them. Aladdin could tell they hadn't eaten in days.

He looked at the bread. He had risked his life to get it—and his mouth was watering like crazy. But he couldn't let them go hungry. With a sigh, he held his half out to the children. "Go on, take it," he said softly.

Abu scowled, but he handed over his piece, too.

The girl smiled. She took Abu's bread and gave his fur a gentle stroke.

Abu liked that. People didn't usually treat him so

nicely. He tipped his hat and strutted away proudly—
and smacked right into Aladdin's legs.

But Aladdin didn't even notice. His eyes were focused
on something straight ahead. "Wow . . . ," Aladdin
muttered.

The marketplace had fallen silent. Right through the
middle rode a man on a horse. He wore robes of the
finest silk, studded with jewels. As the people cleared
the way and bowed, the man thrust his chin proudly in
the air.

Aladdin wandered out of the alley and into the crowd.
Everyone was murmuring about the rich-looking man.

"That's Prince Achmed," a woman said, "on his way
to the palace."

"Just another suitor for the princess," an old man said,
shaking his head. "He'll ask to marry her, and she'll
throw him out—just like all the others."

Aladdin stared in awe. If the princess could reject
someone like that, she must be a pretty amazing girl!

Aladdin felt a tug on his leg. Abu was pulling him
toward the crowd. Aladdin could see a group of poor
children clustering too close to Prince Achmed's horse.
Suddenly the horse bucked, frightening the children, and
the prince shouted, "Out of my way, you filthy brats!"

Angered, Aladdin broke through the crowd and strutted right up to Prince Achmed. "If I were as rich as you," he yelled, "I could afford some manners!"

"Out of my way, you flea-bitten street rat!" Prince Achmed kicked his horse and brushed past Aladdin, knocking him down into the mud.

Burning with anger, Aladdin leapt to his feet and started to run after the prince's horse. "I'm not worthless! I'm not a street rat!" he shouted. He ran all the way to the palace doors. With a loud clang, they slammed shut in his face. "And I don't have fleas!" he shouted at the closed doors.

Prince Achmed never even turned around. Aladdin bowed his head sadly and slumped back into town.

As a chilly darkness settled over Agrabah that night, Aladdin and Abu climbed to the roof of a crumbling old building. There were only a few mats and a couple of worn-out pillows, but to Aladdin and Abu, this was home.

Abu curled up on a pillow and closed his eyes. With a smile, Aladdin covered him with a soft mat. "Someday, Abu, things are going to be different," he said. "We'll be dressed in robes instead of rags. And we'll be inside a palace, looking out—instead of outside look-ing in.''

In the distance, the sultan's palace loomed majesti-cally. ''That'd be the life, huh, Abu! To be rich, live in a palace, and never have any problems at all.''

With a sigh, Aladdin lay down to sleep.

CHAPTER THREE

*Y*eeeooow!"

The scream came from the palace menagerie. It echoed into the throne room, where the sultan covered his ears.

Whack! The door slammed against the throne room wall. In stomped an angry Prince Achmed. "I've never been so insulted!" he shouted. "Good luck marrying *her* off!"

"But . . . but . . . ," the sultan sputtered.

The prince marched right by him and out the other door—revealing a big hole in the seat of his pants.

"Jasmine!" the sultan bellowed. He was a roly-poly old man, happy and kind, and loved by his subjects. Only one person could get him upset—his daughter, Princess Jasmine. He loved her dearly, but she was so . . . stubborn. All he wanted her to do was marry a prince. Every princess did it. But Jasmine? *No.* No one was good enough for her!

He waddled into the palace menagerie. The sound of

13

water was all around, flowing down marble waterways, spouting into pools from hand-carved fountains. It was the most beautiful place in all Agrabah. But the sultan noticed none of that now. "Jasmine!" he called again.

"Rrrrrrr . . . ," came a soft growl.

There was a flash of orange and black. The sultan found himself face-to-face with a tiger, its teeth clamped on to the missing piece of Prince Achmed's pants.

"Confound it, Rajah!" the sultan said, grabbing the ripped material.

Rajah slinked away to the back of the garden, where the sultan's daughter sat at the edge of a fountain. "Oh, Father, Rajah was just playing," she said, gently stroking the tiger. "You were just playing with that overdressed, self-absorbed Prince Achmed, weren't you!" she said to Rajah.

Jasmine was more than beautiful. Princes from miles around risked their life crossing the desert to see her. Each vowed to conquer the world for her love.

But as for Jasmine—well, she'd had enough of half-witted princes and bragging noblemen. If only one of them would show a little intelligence . . . some kindness and honesty and a sense of humor wouldn't hurt, either.

The sultan shook his head. "Dearest, you've got to stop rejecting every suitor. The law says you must be married to a prince by your next birthday. You have only three more days."

"The law is wrong!" Jasmine replied. "Father, I hate being forced to marry. If I do marry, I want it to be for love."

"It's not just the law," the sultan said gently. He hesitated for a minute before continuing. "I'm not going to be around forever, and I just want to make sure you're taken care of."

"But I've never done anything on my own! I've never had any real friends—except you, Rajah," Jasmine said, giving her tiger a pat on the head. "I've never even been outside the palace walls!"

"But Jasmine, you're a princess!" cried the sultan.

"Then maybe I don't *want* to be a princess anymore!"

"*Oooooo!*" The sultan threw up his hands and stomped back into the throne room.

A shadow appeared behind him. It was the tall, thin shadow of a man in a pointed turban, with a parrot on his shoulder. In his right hand was a long staff with a snake head carved at the top.

The sultan turned around. "Ah, Jafar, my most trusted adviser!" he said. "I am in desperate need of your wisdom."

"My life is but to serve you," said Jafar with a tight, thin-lipped smile.

"Jasmine refuses to choose a husband," the sultan said. "I am at my wit's end!"

"*Awk!* Wit's end!" Iago squawked.

The sultan reached into a china bowl and took out a cracker. "Have a cracker, Pretty Polly?" he said.

If there was one thing Iago *hated,* it was eating crackers. Especially the dry, stale ones the sultan had. He practically gagged as the sultan stuffed the crackers into his beak.

"Your Majesty certainly has a way with dumb animals," Jafar remarked. "Now then, I may be able to find a solution to your problem, but it would require the use of the Blue Diamond."

The sultan backed away. He clutched at the ring on his finger.

"My ring has been in the family for years—" he protested.

Jafar held his staff in front of the sultan's eyes. The eyes of the snake head began to glow. "It's necessary

16

to find the princess a suitor, isn't it!" Jafar said, moving closer. "Don't worry . . . everything will be fine."

The sultan could not stop staring at the snake head. His willpower was draining away. "Everything will be fine," he droned as he slipped the ring off his finger and gave it to Jafar.

Jafar smiled. "You are most gracious, my sire," Jafar said. "Now run along and play with your toys, hmmm!"

"Yes . . . ," the sultan said dreamily, waddling away.

Jafar turned and left the throne room. As he hurried down a marble corridor, Iago began spitting out the crackers. "I can't take it anymore! If I have to choke down one more of those moldy, disgusting crackers, I'll grab him by the neck and—"

"Calm yourself, Iago," said Jafar. "This Blue Diamond will reveal to us the Diamond in the Rough— the one who can enter the cave and bring us the lamp."

At the end of the corridor, Jafar entered his private quarters. "Soon *I* will be sultan, not that jumbo portion of stupidity!"

"And then," Iago crowed, "I stuff crackers down *his* throat!"

At the other end of the dark room, Jafar pushed open a secret door, revealing a spiral staircase. He began climbing the stairs that led to his private laboratory. In every corner of the room, potions bubbled in glass beakers. There was a huge cauldron in the back and an enormous hourglass on an old table.

Jafar walked toward the hourglass, holding the Blue Diamond. "Now, Iago, we go to work."

Early the next morning, Jasmine crept to the palace wall. Rajah followed close by, his shoulders slumped in sadness.

"I'm sorry, Rajah," Jasmine said, "but I can't stay here and have my life lived for me."

Tears welled up inside her. It was hard enough running away from her father. But having to look into Rajah's eyes made it more painful than she could have imagined.

She had to make her move now, otherwise she might change her mind. Stepping onto Rajah's back, Jasmine quickly climbed the garden wall. Pausing at the top, she said, "I'll miss you, Rajah. Good-bye."

Then she disappeared over the side, into the land of her subjects—a land she had never visited before.

CHAPTER FOUR

Breakfast is served, Abu!" said Aladdin as he cracked open a ripe, juicy melon. Perched on an awning, the two friends had a perfect view of the bustling marketplace below. All around them, merchants announced their wares. "Buy a pot—brass and silver!" called one.

"Sugared dates and figs!" shouted another as he strolled by a crowd of people watching a fire breather. "Pistachio nuts! Let the fire breather roast them for you!"

"Fresh fish!" cried a third vendor. Aladdin watched as the man waved a large fish high in the air, almost smacking it into the face of a young girl who was covered with a thin cloak. She staggered backward, bumping right into the fire breather. He belched a long plume of fire.

"Oh!" the startled girl cried out. "Excuse me. I'm sorry!"

Aladdin stopped eating. He couldn't help staring.

Maybe it was her eyes, so deep and kind. Or her hair, like a waterfall made of the blackest silk. Or her perfect skin, or her . . .

Aladdin blushed. He *never* thought of girls that way. But this one—well, this one was different. Special somehow. Aladdin watched her as she made her way through the market.

Jasmine spotted a ragged little boy standing in a daze in front of a mound of ripe fruit. "You must be hungry," she said, taking an apple from the cart. "Here you go."

The child beamed. Clutching the apple, he ran away.

"You'd better pay for that!" the vendor said.

"Pay?" Jasmine looked puzzled. She had never paid for anything in her life. "I'm sorry, sir, I don't have any money, but I'm sure I can get some from the sultan—"

"Thief!" The seller grabbed her arm. With his other hand, he pulled out a shiny knife. "Do you know what the penalty is for stealing?"

Suddenly Aladdin darted between them and grabbed the vendor's arm. "Thank you, kind sir, I'm so glad you found my sister!" he said. Turning to Jasmine, he scolded, "I've been looking all over for you!" Jasmine was about to protest when Aladdin whispered, "Just play along. . . ."

The seller pulled Aladdin aside and said, "You know this girl? She said she knew the sultan!"

"She's my sister," Aladdin replied. Then, lowering his voice, he said, "Sadly, she's a little crazy. She thinks the monkey is the sultan."

Quickly Jasmine began bowing to Abu. "O Wise Sultan," she said. "How may I serve you?"

People in the crowd began to laugh. Aladdin helped Jasmine up and said, "Now come along, Sis. Time to see the doctor."

As the seller stared at Aladdin and Jasmine, Abu snatched apples off the cart and stuffed them into his vest.

Jasmine stopped in front of a camel and said, "Hello, Doctor, how are you?"

"No, no, not that one," Aladdin said. "Come on, Sis." He called over his shoulder, "Come on, Sultan!"

Abu followed after them. He puffed out his chest, imitating the sultan—and three apples tumbled out of his vest.

The seller turned red with fury. "Come back here, you little thieves!" he shrieked.

But it was too late. The three of them broke into a run and disappeared into the crowd.

At the palace, Jafar chuckled with evil glee. Iago was frantically turning a wheel that was attached to a generator. Electricity spurted from the generator into a bubbling cauldron. Slowly a shimmering blue cloud formed in the air.

The Blue Diamond was encased in a frame above an enormous hourglass. Jafar swept his arm in front of it, chanting, "Part, sands of time! Reveal to me the one who can enter the cave!"

He flipped the hourglass over. Then, with a loud *crrrack!* a bolt of lightning shot from the cloud. It struck the diamond, which exploded into a pulsing blue light.

The sand in the hourglass began to glow and swirl. Slowly an image began to form—an image of Aladdin running through the marketplace.

"That's the clown we've been waiting for!" Iago blurted out.

"Yes, a ragged little urchin. How perfect—he'll never be missed!" Jafar looked at Iago with a twisted grin. "Let's have the guards extend him an invitation to the palace, shall we?"

Aladdin, Abu, and Jasmine jumped from rooftop to rooftop in the marketplace. Aladdin could tell Jasmine had never been to that part of Agrabah before. But he had to admit one thing—when it came to roof hopping, she was a fast learner.

When Aladdin and Abu finally reached their home, Jasmine looked around and said, "Is this where you live?"

"Yep, just me and Abu," Aladdin replied. "It's not much, but it has a great view." He pointed toward the palace. "Amazing, huh? I wonder what it would be like to live there and have servants and valets—"

Jasmine sighed. "And people who tell you where to go and how to dress."

"That's better than here," Aladdin replied. "Always scraping for food and ducking guards—"

"Never being free to make your own choices," Jasmine said. "Always feeling—"

"*Trapped,*" they said at the same time. Their eyes met, and they smiled. Aladdin blushed, then quickly took an apple from Abu and tossed it to Jasmine. "So where are you from?" he asked, changing the subject.

"What does it matter?" Jasmine answered. "I ran

away, and I'm not going back. My father is forcing me to get married."

"That's awful!" Aladdin said.

Jasmine's eyes met his again. Suddenly Aladdin couldn't speak, couldn't even move. Strange feelings raced around inside him, feelings so strong they made him dizzy. Who *was* this mysterious girl?

Aladdin could hear Abu chattering wildly, but he didn't listen. All he could see, all he could hear, was Jasmine.

"Here you are!" a voice roared.

Aladdin snapped out of his trance. Below them stood a group of the sultan's guards, swords drawn.

"They're after me!" Aladdin and Jasmine said together. They stopped, looking at each other in confusion, then spoke again at the same time: "They're after *you!*"

But there was no time to figure things out. Aladdin looked over the opposite side of the roof. There was a pile of hay below. "Do you trust me?" he asked Jasmine, pulling her close. Their eyes locked again.

"Well . . . yes," she replied.

"Then jump!"

Aladdin, Jasmine, and Abu leapt off the roof. They

landed safely in the hay and quickly got to their feet. Aladdin spun around, ready to sprint for his life.

But it was too late. Rasoul loomed over him, smirking. "We just keep running into each other, eh, street rat! It's the dungeon for you, boy!"

Jasmine stepped in Rasoul's path. "Let him go!"

"Look, a street *mouse!*" Rasoul snarled. With a laugh, he pushed Jasmine to the ground.

Jasmine sprang to her feet. Anger flashed in her eyes. Regally drawing back her hood, she said in a firm, commanding voice, "Unhand him, by order of the princess!"

"The *princess?*" Aladdin repeated.

The guards froze in shock. "Princess Jasmine!" Rasoul said. "What—what are you doing outside the palace?"

"Just do as I command," Jasmine said. "Release him."

"I would, Princess," Rasoul replied, "except my orders come from Jafar. You'll have to take it up with him."

And with a sheepish shrug, he dragged Aladdin away.

"Believe me, I will!" Jasmine exclaimed.

Back at the palace, Jasmine stormed into Jafar's chamber.

There he was, looking as sneaky and sinister as always. "Princess," he said, "how may I be of service?"

Princess Jasmine looked him sharply in the eye. "Jafar, the guards just took a boy from the market—on your orders."

"Your father has charged me with keeping peace in Agrabah," Jafar said. "The boy was a criminal. He tried to kidnap you."

"He didn't *kidnap* me!" Jasmine replied. "I ran away!"

Jafar's brow creased with concern. "Oh dear, how frightfully upsetting. Had I but known . . ." His voice trailed off.

"What do you mean?" Jasmine asked.

"Sadly, the boy's sentence has already been carried out."

Jasmine shuddered. "What sentence?"

Jafar sighed. He put a hand on Jasmine's shoulder. "Death," Jafar said softly. "By beheading."

A gasp caught in Jasmine's throat. "How . . . how *could* you?"

She turned and ran out, not stopping until she reached the menagerie.

Rajah bounded happily toward her, but Jasmine ran

right by him. She collapsed by a fountain, tears running down her cheek.

Do you trust me? the boy had asked her. Yes, she had. This boy was so different from the others—funny, kind, friendly. . . .

And now he was dead. Because of a stupid mistake.

"Oh, Rajah," she said. "This is all my fault. I didn't even know his name."

Jasmine buried her head in Rajah's fur and wept.

CHAPTER FIVE

*T*he palace dungeon was cold, dark, and dirty. Not even the sultan had ever entered it. All prisoners were brought there by Jafar—and not one had escaped.

Aladdin was determined to be the first. He grunted loudly, struggling at his chains, but they held fast to the stone wall.

Jafar had lied to Jasmine. Aladdin was alive—but not for long, if everything went according to Jafar's plan.

Aladdin collapsed to the floor with a sigh. "She was the *princess*," he said to himself. "I can't believe it!"

Just then a shadow appeared on the wall—the shadow of a small monkey poised between the bars of the prison window. "Abu!" Aladdin cried, spinning around. "Down here!"

Abu hopped down. He frowned at Aladdin and chattered angrily as he did an imitation of a pretty girl walking.

Aladdin knew he was being scolded for paying too

much attention to Jasmine. "Hey, she was in trouble," he said. "I'll never see her again, anyway. I'm a street rat, remember? Besides, there's some law that says she's got to marry a prince." He exhaled with frustration. "She deserves a prince."

Abu pulled a small pick out of his vest pocket and unlocked Aladdin's cuffs. Grinning with triumph, he pulled Aladdin toward the window.

But Aladdin just slumped to the floor. He was still thinking of Jasmine. "I'm a fool," he said.

"You're only a fool if you give up," came a crackly voice.

Aladdin turned to see an old snaggletoothed man hobble out of the shadows. His white beard hung to the floor, and he had a hump on his back. He looked as though he had been in the dungeon for years. "Who are you?" Aladdin asked.

"I am a lowly prisoner like yourself—but together, perhaps we can be more. I know of a cave filled with treasures beyond your wildest dreams." The man shuffled closer, smiling. "There's treasure enough to impress your princess, I'd wager."

Abu's eyes lit up at the mention of treasure. He tugged at Aladdin's vest.

Neither of them saw Iago peek out of the old man's hump and whisper, "Jafar, could you hurry up? I'm dying in here!"

Aladdin gave the prisoner a forlorn look. "But the law says she has to marry—"

Jafar cut Aladdin off. He raised a bony finger and spoke once again in an old man's voice. "You've heard of the Golden Rule? Whoever has the gold makes the rules!"

"Why would you share this treasure with me?" Aladdin asked.

"I need a young pair of legs and a strong back to go in after it." Jafar walked to the dungeon wall and pushed one of the stones. Slowly an entire section of wall opened, revealing a hidden stairway. "So, do we have a deal?"

Aladdin was hesitant, but he shook the old man's hand.

Jafar cackled with excitement. "We're off!"

It was dark by the time they reached the Cave of Wonders. Jafar took out the scarab pieces and fit them together once again.

Aladdin stared in awe as the pieces flew into the sandstone and the massive tiger-god arose.

"*Who disturbs my slumber?*" the intimidating voice boomed. Jafar motioned for Aladdin to go closer.

Abu jumped into Aladdin's vest. Aladdin tried to keep from trembling. "Uh, it is I . . . Aladdin."

A tunnel of harsh light shot from the tiger-god's mouth. Aladdin had to turn away. "*Proceed,*" the voice continued. "*Touch nothing but the lamp.*"

"Quickly, my boy," Jafar urged in his old man's voice. "Fetch the lamp, and then you shall have your reward!"

Cautiously Aladdin stepped inside the tiger-god's mouth. Through the blinding light, he saw a long stairway leading downward. At the bottom there were mountains of gold. *Cascades* of gold. Coins, jewels, plates, bowls, goblets, chests, all piled together as far as he could see.

Abu was practically hypnotized by the sight of all that gold and went straight for an enormous treasure chest.

"Abu!" Aladdin warned. "Don't touch *anything!* We have to find that lamp."

Abu grumbled, but turned from the chest and followed his master through the cave—until he sensed a strange movement behind him. He spun around to look.

Nothing—just a purple carpet with gold tassels, lying on the floor. Abu turned and ran toward Aladdin.

This time something tapped Abu on the shoulder, then snatched his hat. Abu spun around again.

It was the carpet, walking along behind him.

"Eeeeeeeeeee!" Abu shrieked, jumping on Aladdin for protection.

In fright, the carpet quickly ran behind a large pile of coins.

"Cut it out, Abu!" Aladdin said.

Abu jabbered away, pointing to the large mound. Aladdin turned and saw a tassel stick out, then quickly pull itself in.

Aladdin moved closer for a better look. He could see the carpet moving away from him. "A magic carpet!" he said. Then he called, "Come on out, we're not going to hurt you."

Using its two lower tassels as legs and its upper ones as hands, the carpet slowly emerged and handed Aladdin Abu's hat. Aladdin's mouth hung open in disbelief.

Abu snatched the hat and began scolding the carpet.

The carpet slowly walked away, drooped over in shame. "Hey, wait a minute, don't go!" Aladdin said. "Maybe you can help us find this lamp. . . ."

The carpet whirled around and began pointing excitedly. Aladdin grinned. "I think he knows where it is!"

Rising off the ground, the carpet began to fly. Aladdin and Abu followed it into another cavern.

Aladdin stopped in his tracks. This cavern made the other one look like a waiting room. It stretched upward so high Aladdin couldn't see the ceiling. The walls were a cool blue, unlike any color he had ever seen in the desert. A lagoon of aqua blue water stretched from wall to wall.

In the center of the lake stood a tower of solid rock with only a series of stepping stones leading to it. On top, lit by a magical beam of light, was a small object.

It was too far away to see, but Aladdin knew that it must be the lamp. His heart began to race. It wouldn't be easy to get to the top. First he would have to hopscotch across the rocks, then he would have to climb the steep, jagged tower of rock.

"Wait here," he said to Abu and the carpet. "And remember, don't touch *anything*."

Springing from stone to stone, Aladdin arrived at the base of the tower. With a sudden groan, the sloping rock transformed into a staircase.

Aladdin smiled. Someone—some*thing*—was on his side. He raced upward, two steps at a time.

At the top, the lamp came into clear view.

It was dusty and dented and cheaper looking than the worst used lamp he had ever seen in the marketplace.

Aladdin picked it up. "This is it?" he said to himself. "This is what we came all the way here for?"

Out of the corner of his eye, he spotted Abu and the carpet. They were in front of a large golden statue that looked like a giant monkey idol. Its arms were outstretched, and in its cupped palms it held an enormous red jewel.

And Abu was reaching right for it.

"Abu!" Aladdin shouted. "*No!*"

But it was too late. Abu had the jewel in his hands.

The ground began to rumble instantly. Rocks and dust fell from above. The voice of the tiger-god echoed like a cannon: *"Infidels! You have touched the forbidden treasures! Now you shall never again see the light of day!"*

The jewel began to melt in Abu's hand. Panicked, he put it back into the palms of the statue.

But the damage was already done. The stairway beneath Aladdin transformed into a long chute, and his feet gave way.

With a last-minute lunge, Aladdin grabbed the lamp. Tumbling down the chute, he saw the lagoon become a pool of boiling lava. He closed his eyes, bracing himself for the end.

Whoosh! He stopped in midair. Something was pushing him upward. His eyes sprang open.

The carpet had caught him, and it was whisking him away!

The cavern shook violently. Aladdin held tightly to the carpet. It dodged right and left as large rocks fell from the ceiling. Aladdin looked down, searching for Abu.

"Eeeeee!" came a cry from below. There he was, hopping across the stepping-stones and screeching. Over his head, a boulder hurtled toward him.

With a burst of speed, the carpet streaked down. Aladdin plucked Abu away from danger, then flew toward the cavern entrance. The ground below erupted as the piles of dazzling treasures burst into flames. Aladdin and Abu looked down in horror. The coins and jewels were melting!

The carpet raced to the stairway, charred by a wave of lava. They could see the starry night sky through the entrance above. Just a few more feet . . .

Thunk! A jagged piece of rock fell onto the carpet, pinning it to the ground.

Aladdin and Abu tumbled onto the stairs.

Aladdin looked down at the carpet in dismay. There was no way he could save it. It would be hard enough to save himself.

He looked up. He could see the opening at the top—freedom. Abu scaled the steps and hopped outside.

Aladdin followed as fast as he could, but the stairs began to shake. He lost his footing.

Springing to his feet, he lunged for the top step. His fingers clutched on to it—just as the entire stairway buckled beneath him.

Aladdin dangled over the collapsing cave. "Help me!" he cried. "I can't hold on!"

Still dressed as the beggar, Jafar peeked over the edge. "First give me the lamp!"

There was no time to argue. Aladdin held it out.

Jafar's eyes gleamed as he grabbed the lamp and stuffed it into his robe. "At last!" he shrieked in triumph. Leering at Aladdin, he pulled out a dagger.

"What are you doing?" Aladdin cried.

"Giving you your reward!" Jafar replied. "Your *eternal* reward!"

Abu leapt at Jafar, biting him hard on the arm.

"Yeeeeaggggh!" Jafar screamed. He fought hard, but Abu held tight.

Finally Jafar dropped the dagger. With a furious gesture, he flung Abu into the cave.

Aladdin's fingers could hold on no longer. He let go.

The walls of the cavern raced by him as he and Abu fell head over heels.

CHAPTER SIX

A laddin awoke on the cave floor. The fire was out, the lava gone; only the steady drip of water echoed throughout the cave.

On top of him lay the carpet and Abu.

Aladdin groaned and sat up. The carpet fell off, and Abu began to stir. Above him, Aladdin could see no opening, only the solid ceiling of the cavern.

"We're trapped," he said. "That two-faced son of a jackal! He's long gone with that lamp."

Abu jumped up. Something bulged in his vest—a jewel, Aladdin figured. Like a magician, Abu waved his arms, reached into his vest, and pulled out the hidden object.

Aladdin blinked and shook his head. It was the lamp!

"Why, you little thief," Aladdin said with a smile. He took the beat-up lamp and studied it carefully. "There's something written on it, but it's hard to make out."

Aladdin rubbed the faded words with his sleeve. It

was almost impossible to get the grime off. He rubbed harder and harder—then suddenly stopped.

The lamp was glowing!

Aladdin gasped. Abu and the carpet backed away.

Then . . . *Poooof!* Colorful smoke erupted from the lamp's spout. It whirled crazily, growing into a blue cloud, slowly forming into a shape—an enormous flowing shape with arms, a chest, a head, and a wild-eyed face with a long, black, curling beard.

"Ten thousand years will give you *such* a crick in the neck!" the blue creature said.

Aladdin and Abu watched as he then grabbed his own head and twisted it all the way around. "Wow, does that feel good!" he said. "Nice to be back, ladies and gentlemen. Hi! What's your name?"

"Uh . . . Aladdin."

"Hello, Aladdin! Can I call you Al? Or maybe just Din? Or how about Laddie? 'Here, boy! Come on, Laddie!' " He whistled and pretended to call a dog. Then, in another puff of blue smoke, he *became* a giant dog.

His eyes wide, Aladdin turned to the carpet. "I must have hit my head harder than I thought."

The creature changed back to his original form. "Say, you're a lot smaller than my last master!" he said.

"Wait a minute," Aladdin said. "I'm your *master?*"

"That's right! And I am your genie, direct from the lamp! Right here for your wish fulfillment! Three wishes, to be exact—and *ixnay* on the wishing for more wishes! *Three,* that's it! No substitutions, exchanges, or refunds!"

"Three wishes!" Aladdin said. "Any three I want?"

"Uh, almost," the genie replied. "There are a few limitations. Rule number one—I can't kill anybody, so don't ask. Rule number two—I can't make anybody fall in love with anybody else. Rule number three—I can't bring people back from the dead. Other than that, you got it!"

Aladdin liked this genie. He decided to tease him a little. "Limitations?" He sighed. "Some all-powerful genie. I don't know, Abu, he probably can't even get us out of this cave."

The genie put his hands on his hips. "Excuse me? You don't believe me?" Jumping onto the carpet, he scooped up Aladdin and Abu in his mammoth hands. "You're getting your wishes, so sit down, and we are out of here!"

He put them down, then swung his arm overhead. A thunderous boom resounded above them, and a crack opened in the cavern's ceiling. Rocks and sand fell aside, and early morning light poured in.

The carpet began to rise. It spiraled upward, picking up speed. Aladdin held tight as the genie reared back and let loose a laugh that shook the walls.

Aladdin couldn't keep from laughing himself. The desert air never smelled so good.

He was free.

And he still had his three wishes left.

CHAPTER SEVEN

*J*afar, this is an outrage!" the sultan yelled, pacing the throne room. "From now on, you're to discuss sentencing of prisoners with me—*before* they are beheaded!"

Princess Jasmine scowled at Jafar as he bowed his head. On his shoulder, even Iago looked sorry. "My humblest apologies to both of you," Jafar said.

"At least *some* good will come of my being forced to marry," Jasmine said. "When I am queen, I will have the power to get rid of *you,* Jafar!" With that, she stalked out to the menagerie.

"Jasmine!" the sultan called, running after her.

Jafar watched them leave. His sad, sorrowful look began to disappear. All his rage and frustration bubbled up. "If only I had gotten that lamp," he muttered through clenched teeth.

"To think we've got to keep kissing up to that chump and his chump daughter the rest of our lives," Iago said.

"Until she finds a chump *husband*," Jafar remarked. "Then she'll have us banished—or beheaded!"

"Wait a minute, Jafar!" Iago said. "What if *you* marry the princess! Then you become the sultan, right!"

Jafar walked slowly to the throne and sat down. It felt *wonderful!* "Hmmmm," he said. "The idea has merit. . . ."

"Yeah!" Iago squawked. "And then we drop papa-in-law and the little woman off a cliff—ker-*splat!*"

Jafar burst out laughing. "I love the way your foul little mind works!"

In a desert oasis just outside Agrabah, the carpet swooped down to the sand. The genie turned to Aladdin with a proud grin. "Well, how about that, huh! Do you doubt me now!"

"Nope," Aladdin said. "Now, about my three wishes . . ."

"Three!" the genie said. "You are down by one, boy!"

Aladdin smiled mischievously. "I never actually *wished* to get out of the cave. You did that on your own!"

The genie thought for a moment. "All right," he said with a laugh. "You win. But no more freebies!"

Aladdin hopped off the carpet and began pacing around. "Hmm . . . three wishes . . . What would *you* wish for?"

"Me? No one's ever asked me that before." The genie thought it over for a moment. "Well, in my case . . . freedom."

"You mean, you're a prisoner?" Aladdin asked.

"That's what being a genie's all about." The genie shrugged. "Phenomenal cosmic powers, itty-bitty living space."

The carpet, Abu, and Aladdin peered inside the small lamp. "Genie, that's terrible," Aladdin said.

"To be free, to be my own master—that would be greater than all the magic and all the treasures in the world." The genie sighed. "But the only way I can get out is for my master to wish me out, so you can guess how often that's happened."

Aladdin thought about this for a moment. "I'll do it," he finally said. "I'll set you free."

"Yeah, right," the genie said, rolling his eyes.

"No, I'm not lying," Aladdin said. "I promise—after

my first two wishes, I'll use my third wish to set you free."

"Okay, here's hoping!" said the genie. "Now, what is it *you* want?"

"Well," Aladdin said, "there's this girl—"

"Wrong! I can't make anyone fall in love, remember?"

"But Genie, she's smart and fun and beautiful. . . ." Aladdin shrugged and looked at the ground. "But she's the princess. To even have a chance, I'd have to be—"

That was it! The answer was right in front of him! "Hey!" Aladdin said. "Can you make me . . . a prince?"

The genie raised an eyebrow. "Is that an official wish? Say the magic words. . . ."

"Genie, I wish for you to make me a prince!" Aladdin blurted.

"*All right!*" The genie began circling around Aladdin. "Now, first we have to get rid of the fez-and-vest combo." With a sweeping gesture, he conjured up a robe of fine silk and a turban with a dazzling jewel and shining gold trim. "Ooh, I like it!"

"Wow!" Aladdin could hardly believe how . . . *princely* he looked. No one would dare call him "street rat" now. He picked up the lamp and hid it under his turban. No decent prince would dare be seen with such a piece of junk.

"Hmmm, you'll need some transportation. . . ." The genie looked at Abu. "Uh, excuse me! Monkey boy!"

Abu shot away, trying to hide. But it was no use. With a snap of his fingers, the genie turned him into a camel. "Hmmm . . . not good enough," the genie said, snapping his fingers again. This time Abu appeared as a magnificent stallion. "Still not enough. . . ." With a decisive snap, Abu was transformed again, this time into an elephant. "What better way to make your entrance down the streets of Agrabah than riding your very own elephant! Talk about trunk space!"

Aladdin could do nothing but stare, dumbfounded. The genie was on a roll. He gestured wildly, laughing at the top of his lungs. "Hang on to your turban, kid!" he shouted. "We're going to make you a star!"

CHAPTER EIGHT

*J*afar rushed into the throne room, holding a large scroll. "Sire," he called to the sultan, "I have found a solution to the problem with your daughter!"

"*Awk!*" squawked Iago. "Problem with your daughter!"

"It's right here." Jafar unfurled the scroll and began reading: " 'If a princess has not chosen a husband by her sixteenth birthday, then the sultan shall choose for her'!"

The sultan nodded. "But Jasmine hated all those suitors. How can I choose someone she might hate?"

"Not to worry, there is more," Jafar said, unrolling the scroll further. " 'In the event a suitable prince cannot be found, a princess may be wed to—' Hmmm, interesting . . ."

"What?" the sultan demanded. "Who?"

" 'The royal vizier.' " Jafar looked up. "Why, that's *me!*"

"But I thought the law says only a prince can marry a princess," the sultan said, reaching for the scroll.

Jafar quickly set it on a table and picked up his staff. "Desperate times call for desperate measures, my lord."

The snake head began to glow with hypnotic light. "Yes," the sultan said, his eyes glazing over. "Desperate times . . ."

"You will order the princess to marry me," Jafar said confidently.

"I will order the princess to—"

Ra-ta-ta-taaaaaah! The sound of trumpets blared in through the window. The sultan blinked and turned toward the noise. "Wha—what! I heard something!"

Instantly the spell was broken. The sultan rushed to the window and looked out. Muttering, Jafar followed.

A huge band was marching down the main street. A giant peacock float moved slowly behind; lions and bears in colorful painted cages rolled by. People filled the streets to see the grand procession approaching.

"Make way for Prince Ali Ababwa!" the bandleader sang. Behind him strode a majestic elephant, its trunk held proudly in the air. On its back, a canopy bounced up and down.

From the canopy, Aladdin grinned and waved. The crowd roared with admiration. Dancers whirled around him, swordsmen marched in perfect step, and dozens of attendants walked alongside. Abu lumbered on proudly, and the carpet made a perfect cushion for Aladdin on Abu's bumpy back.

The genie floated among the crowd, changing himself every few minutes into a drum major, a harem girl, an old man, a child. In each disguise, he told everyone what a splendid prince was approaching.

By the time Aladdin got to the palace gates, he was the talk of Agrabah. His entire entourage—Abu, swordsmen, brass band, dancers, and all—marched right into the throne room.

As the sultan and Jafar stared, Aladdin slid off Abu's back and onto the carpet. "Your Majesty," Aladdin said, bowing in front of the sultan, "I have journeyed from afar to seek your daughter's hand."

"Prince Ali Ababwa!" the sultan said with a bright smile. "I'm delighted to meet you. This is my royal vizier, Jafar."

Jafar did not look delighted at all. "I'm afraid, Prince Abooboo—"

"Ababwa," Aladdin corrected him.

"Whatever," Jafar said. "You cannot just parade in here uninvited and—"

"What a remarkable device!" the sultan exclaimed, looking at the carpet. "May I try?"

"Why, certainly, Your Majesty!" Aladdin said. He helped the sultan onto the carpet. It took off, flying the sultan around the room.

As the old man hooted with delight, Jafar eyed Aladdin suspiciously. "Just where did you say you were from?"

Before Aladdin could answer, the carpet swooped down and let the sultan off. "Well, this is a very impressive youth, and a prince, besides!" Lowering his voice, the sultan said to Jafar, "If we're lucky, you won't have to marry Jasmine after all!"

"I don't trust him—" Jafar said.

The sultan ignored him. "Yes, Jasmine will like this one."

"And I'm sure I'll like Princess Jasmine," Aladdin said.

"Your Highness!" Jafar blurted. "On Jasmine's behalf, I must say—"

"Just let her meet me," Aladdin interrupted. "*I* will win your daughter."

None of them had seen Jasmine enter from the menagerie, with Rajah behind her. "How dare you!" she said. "Standing around, deciding my future. I am not a prize to be won!" With that, she turned and stormed out.

Aladdin's heart sank. He was sure she'd like him as a prince. He never thought *this* would happen.

"Don't worry, Prince Ali," the sultan said. "Just give her time to cool down. She'll warm to you."

Aladdin and the sultan walked into the menagerie. Jafar watched them silently, then turned to Iago. "I think it's time to say bye-bye to Prince Abooboo. . . ."

CHAPTER NINE

*F*or the rest of the day, Aladdin waited in the menagerie. Jasmine's room was overhead, but she refused to come to her balcony.

As night fell, Aladdin began to give up hope. "What am I going to do!" he moaned. "I should have known I couldn't pull off this stupid prince act."

Abu looked at his master and swung his trunk in sympathy.

"All right," the genie said, looking up from a game of chess with the carpet. "Here's the deal. If you want to court her, you have to tell her the truth. Just be yourself!"

"No way!" Aladdin said. "If Jasmine found out I was really some crummy street rat, she'd laugh at me." He looked up at Jasmine's balcony and drew himself up straight. "I'm going to go see her," he said. "I've got to be smooth. Cool. Confident."

The genie sighed. He knew Aladdin was in for trouble.

The carpet slid beneath Aladdin, lifting him up to Jasmine's balcony. Through her window, Aladdin could see her playing with Rajah. "Princess Jasmine!" he called out.

Jasmine turned and walked to the window. "Who's there?"

"It's me," said Aladdin. Then, remembering his Prince Ali voice, he added, "Prince Ali Ababwa."

"I do not want to see you!" Jasmine snapped.

As she turned back into the room, Aladdin stepped off the carpet and onto the balcony. "Please, Princess, give me a chance!"

Rajah leapt into his path. Aladdin jerked away, almost losing his turban.

Jasmine narrowed her eyes. "Wait. Do I know you? You remind me of someone I met in the marketplace."

Aladdin backed into the shadows. "The marketplace! Why, I have *servants* who go to the marketplace for me! So it couldn't have been me you met."

"No, I guess not," Jasmine said, looking disappointed.

A bee buzzed by Aladdin's ear. He moved to swat it until he heard it speak—in the genie's voice! "Enough about you," he said. "Talk about *her!*"

"Princess Jasmine, you're—uh, beautiful," Aladdin said.

"Rich, too," she said. "And the daughter of the sultan."

Aladdin smiled. "I know."

"A fine prize for any prince to marry," she said, playing along.

"Right! A prince like me!"

"Right! A prince like you!" Jasmine repeated. "And every other swaggering peacock I've met. Go jump off a balcony!"

Jasmine turned and strode into her chamber.

"Mayday! Mayday!" the genie said, still disguised as a bee. "Stop her! Want me to sting her!"

"Buzz off!" Aladdin replied.

"Okay," the genie said. "But remember—*bee* yourself!"

"Yeah, right," Aladdin muttered as the genie flew under his turban and into the lamp.

Jasmine looked over her shoulder. "What?"

"Uh . . . I said, you're *right!*" Aladdin sighed. "You . . . aren't just some prize to be won. You should be free to make your own choice."

Dejected, Aladdin turned away. He climbed over the railing and stepped off the balcony into space.

"No!" Jasmine cried. But Aladdin didn't fall—he was hovering in midair.

"How are you doing that?" Jasmine said, stunned.

"It's, uh, a magic carpet," Aladdin said.

Jasmine looked over the railing and touched the carpet. "It's lovely."

"You don't want to go for a ride . . . do you?" Aladdin gave her a hopeful look. "We could fly away and see the world. . . ."

"Is it safe?" Jasmine asked.

"Sure." Aladdin held out his hand and smiled. "Do you trust me?"

Do you trust me? Jasmine had heard those exact words before, said in the same way. "Yes," she said softly, taking his hand.

She stepped onto the carpet, and it took off. Losing her balance, she fell into Aladdin's arms. He blushed, but he liked the feeling—and he could tell Jasmine did, too.

The carpet soared over the palace. Agrabah stretched out below them, a cluster of twinkling lights. And above them, the stars of the desert sky winked a thousand times as they glided over the sands. In the distance, the sea seemed to be made of the blackest ink.

Swooping among the pyramids, Aladdin and Jasmine whooped with joy. When the carpet flew through an apple orchard, Aladdin reached way out and grabbed an apple for the princess.

He flipped it to her with a lopsided smile. The casual flip; the smile; *Do you trust me?*—all of it was exactly like the boy in the marketplace. Was it possible?

She decided to find out. The carpet finally set them down on the roof of a tall pagoda, and they watched a fireworks display in the distance. "It's all so . . . magical," Jasmine said. "It's a shame Abu had to miss this."

"Nah," Aladdin said. "He hates fireworks. He doesn't really like to fly—"

Aladdin caught himself in midsentence.

"It *is* you!" Jasmine blurted. "Why did you lie to me? Did you think I wouldn't figure it out?"

"No! I mean, I *hoped* you wouldn't—that's not what I meant—" Aladdin groped for words. His stomach churned. He *couldn't* let Jasmine know the truth. "Um . . . the truth is, I sometimes dress as a commoner,

The evil Jafar prepares to fit the halves of an ancient scarab together. Then he can find the Cave of Wonders and the magic lamp hidden there.

Tired of having decisions made for her, the sultan's daughter, Princess Jasmine, tells her beloved pet, Rajah, that she is running away from the palace.

Aladdin shares the morning's meal with his pet monkey, Abu.

Aladdin shows his new friend the view of the sultan's palace, but the disguised princess is not impressed.

Disguised as an old beggar, Jafar tells Aladdin about a cave that conceals a magic lamp and an abundance of treasures — treasures that could be Aladdin's if he retrieves the lamp.

Inside the Cave of Wonders, Abu finds that he is being followed by a magic carpet!

Aladdin reaches the top of the tower and gazes at the ordinary looking lamp that Jafar has sent him to retrieve.

Even though he was told not to touch anything, Abu reaches for a giant jewel.

Aladdin reaches for the lamp just before the cave walls — and the stairs beneath him — crumble.

Aladdin rubs the lamp, and much to his surprise, a giant blue genie pops out and offers to grant him three wishes!

To demonstrate his amazing powers, the genie puts on quite a show for Aladdin, Abu, and the carpet.

The genie tells Aladdin that along with his phenomenal cosmic powers comes an "itty-bitty living space."

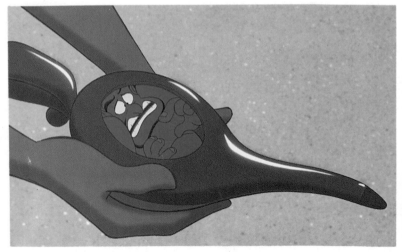

Aladdin's first wish comes true — he's now Prince Ali!

Abu takes a look at his new self.

Jafar uses his snake staff to hypnotize the sultan.

Prince Ali stands majestically atop the carpet and Abu as he rides right into the throne room!

to escape the pressures of palace life. Yeah. But I really am Prince Ali Ababwa!"

Jasmine looked unsure. "Why didn't you just tell me?"

"Well, you know . . . royalty going into the city in disguise . . . sounds a little strange, don't you think?"

Perfect! He knew he had her now. After all, *she* had been in disguise when he met her.

"Not that strange," she said, resting her chin on Aladdin's shoulder.

Together they watched the fireworks until they were too tired to keep their eyes open. The carpet then flew them back to the palace, hovering outside Jasmine's window.

Jasmine stepped onto the balcony, then turned toward Aladdin. They smiled at each other over the railing—until the carpet gave Aladdin a gentle nudge forward.

His lips suddenly met hers. She didn't move a bit. In the soft light of the stars, they shared a long kiss.

"Good night, my handsome prince," she said, backing into her chamber.

"Sleep well, Princess," Aladdin replied.

As she disappeared behind a curtain, Aladdin

grinned. "For the first time in my life," he murmured dreamily as the carpet floated down to the garden, "things are starting to go right."

He snapped back to reality when he felt the hard grip of rough hands on his shoulder. Turning around, Aladdin came face-to-face with Rasoul.

Before Aladdin could move, another guard slapped manacles on his wrists and ankles. Rasoul stuffed a gag in his throat.

"Abu!" Aladdin tried to yell through the gag. "Abu, help!"

He looked around wildly until he spotted Abu—hanging from a tree, tied up with thick rope. The carpet tried to fly away, but another guard threw it into a cage.

Jafar emerged from the shadows. On his shoulder, Iago was grinning. "I'm afraid you've worn out your welcome, Prince Abooboo," Jafar hissed.

Aladdin whirled around. He struggled with his chains. If only he could reach his turban. The lamp was underneath—and the genie was inside the lamp.

Jafar looked calmly at the guards. "Make sure he is never found."

CHAPTER TEN

*I*n the chill of the desert night, the guards rushed Aladdin to the sea by camel. And without a word, they pushed him over a cliff.

Aladdin plunged into the water with a loud splash. In the dim moonlight, he could see his turban floating away. The lamp slowly emerged, then dropped to the seafloor.

He kicked his legs, desperate to reach the lamp. He groped with his hands. . . . There—he had it. But his strength was leaving him. He tried to rub the lamp, but he was weak . . . so weak . . .

Sploosh! The genie materialized, wearing a shower cap and holding a scrub brush. "Never fails," he said. "You get in the bath, and there's a rub at the lamp. Hello!"

Instantly his smile disappeared. Aladdin was limp.

"Al! Kid! Snap out of it!" the genie pleaded, grabbing Aladdin. "I can't help you unless you make a wish. You have to say, 'Genie, I want you to save my life!' Got it?''

Aladdin's head bobbed ever so slightly.

''I'll take that as a yes!'' The genie let go of Aladdin and swam in a circle. A whirlpool formed, spinning Aladdin upward.

He burst through the surface, coughing and flailing. Before he could fall, the genie scooped him up and flew away. ''Don't scare me like that!'' the genie scolded.

Aladdin looked around with excitement. He was alive—wet and humiliated, but alive. As they flew back toward Agrabah, Aladdin looked into the smiling face of his rescuer.

''Genie, I . . . Thanks'' was all he could say.

Jasmine had never been happier. She couldn't stop humming, and she couldn't stop thinking about Aladdin.

As she unbraided her hair in the bedroom mirror, she didn't notice her father walk in, with Jafar behind him. ''Jasmine . . . ,'' the sultan began.

She turned around. ''Oh, Father! I just had the most wonderful time. I'm so happy!''

The sultan stared straight ahead. ''You should be,

Jasmine," he said in a dull voice. "I have chosen a husband for you. You will marry Jafar."

Jasmine gasped.

Jafar stepped forward. The snake head of his staff glowed brightly, working its hypnotic spell on the sultan.

"Never!" Jasmine said. "Father, I choose Prince Ali!"

Jafar laughed. "Prince Ali left, like all the others. But don't worry. Wherever he went, I'm sure he made quite a splash."

"Better check your crystal ball, Jafar!" came a voice from the window.

Jafar turned. Iago squawked in surprise. It was Aladdin!

Jasmine ran to him. "Prince Ali!" she cried. "Are you all right?"

"Yes," Aladdin said, "but no thanks to Jafar. He tried to have me killed!"

"Your Highness," Jafar said, "he's obviously lying."

"Obviously . . . lying . . . ," the sultan repeated mechanically.

"Papa, what's wrong with you?" Jasmine said with dismay.

Aladdin leapt across the room toward Jafar. "I know

what's wrong!" He pried the staff loose from Jafar and smashed the snake head on the floor.

"Oh! Oh my . . . ," the sultan said, shaking his head. "I feel so strange."

"Your Highness," Aladdin said, holding the broken staff in the air. "Jafar's been controlling you with this!"

The sultan's eyes narrowed. "Jafar? You—you traitor! Guards! Arrest Jafar at once!"

But Jafar had caught sight of something he hadn't noticed before—peeking out of Aladdin's turban was the magic lamp! He lunged for it, but the sultan's guards seized him.

"This is not done yet, boy!" Jafar said. Reaching into his robe, he pulled out a magic pellet and threw it on the floor. In a puff of smoke, he and Iago were gone.

"Find him!" the sultan yelled to his guards. "I can't believe it—Jafar, my trusted counselor, plotting against me!"

His shocked expression changed to a smile when he turned back to Jasmine and Aladdin. "Can it be! My daughter has finally chosen a suitor!"

Jasmine nodded, and the sultan threw his arms around Aladdin. "Oh, you brilliant boy! You two will be wed at once! You'll be happy, prosperous—and then you, my boy, will become sultan!"

Sultan! Aladdin swallowed nervously. This was supposed to be the happiest moment of his life, but he was suddenly very worried.

Iago flew around Jafar's lab in a blind panic. "We've got to get out of here!" he said. "I've got to pack!"

But Jafar was deep in thought. He burst out with a sudden laugh and gripped Iago by the throat. "Prince Ali is nothing more than that ragged urchin Aladdin!" he said. "He has the *lamp,* Iago!"

Iago's eyes narrowed. "Why, that little, cheating—"

"But *you* are going to relieve him of it!" Jafar said with a sinister grin. "Listen closely."

Iago leaned in as Jafar whispered his master plan.

CHAPTER ELEVEN

*A*laddin was given the most comfortable suite in the palace, but he barely slept that night.

By dawn he was pacing back and forth, holding his turban, the lamp inside. Abu and the carpet sat outside by the window, watching him with concern.

"Huzzah!" the genie cried, popping out of the lamp. "Aladdin, you've just won the heart of the princess! What are you going to do next!" He lowered his voice to a whisper. "Psst. Your next line is, 'I'm going to free the genie'!"

"Genie," Aladdin said sadly, "I'm sorry, but I can't. They want to make me sultan—no, they want to make *Prince Ali* sultan. The only reason anyone thinks I'm worth anything is because of you! What if they find out the truth! What if Jasmine finds out! She'll hate me." Aladdin looked into the genie's pale, disappointed face. "Genie, I need you. Without you, I'm just Aladdin."

The genie tried to control his anger. "I understand.

After all, you've lied to everyone else. Hey, I was beginning to feel left out. Now, if you'll excuse me. . . ."

With that, he disappeared into the lamp.

"Genie," Aladdin called out, "I'm really sorry."

The genie's lips stuck out of the spout and razzed him.

"Fine!" Aladdin snapped, throwing a pillow over the lamp. "Then just stay in there!" As he stomped away, he could see Abu and the carpet watching him from the window. "What are you guys looking at!"

As Abu and the carpet turned away, Jasmine's voice came from the menagerie. "Ali! Will you please come here! Hurry!"

"Coming, Jasmine!" Aladdin called out the window.

He rushed outside. As he ran to the menagerie in the direction of Jasmine's voice, he passed a group of flamingos in a pond.

At least they all *looked* like flamingos.

Iago snickered to himself. His imitation of Jasmine had worked—and his flamingo disguise was perfect, thanks to Jafar's magic. When Aladdin was gone, he hurried into the empty room and quickly stole the lamp. Hooking it with his beak, he flew outside and straight back to Jafar's lab.

"Ali! There you are," said Jasmine. "I've been looking all over for you!"

Aladdin turned around, puzzled. Abu and the carpet scampered to his side. Jasmine was running toward him. But how could she have been "looking all over" when she had just—

"Hurry," she said, taking him by the hand. "Father's about to make the wedding announcement."

They climbed the stairs of a tower that overlooked the courtyard. Townspeople clogged every square inch trying desperately to see the royal couple. Jasmine stepped onto the platform and took her place next to her father. Smiling, the sultan announced to the crowd: "Ladies and gentlemen, my daughter has chosen a suitor—Prince Ali Ababwa!"

CHAPTER TWELVE

*H*igh in another tower that overlooked the courtyard, Jafar and Iago watched as Aladdin was about to step before the roaring crowd.

"Look at them cheering that little pip-squeak," cried Iago.

"Let them cheer," Jafar said as he held the lamp tightly and began to rub it. "At last," he said. "The power is mine!"

In a puff of smoke, the genie appeared. "Al, if you're going to apologize, I—" The genie's jaw dropped when he saw Jafar.

"*I* am your master now!" Jafar said.

"I was afraid of that—"

"Keep quiet!" snapped Jafar. "And now, slave, grant me my first wish. I wish to be sultan!"

As Aladdin stared down from the platform, the crowd suddenly became hazy. Clouds swirled over the palace, and with a loud tearing sound, the canopy over the platform was ripped off. Jasmine and Aladdin looked around in confusion as a strange magical light engulfed the sultan. And when it stopped, the sultan was on the floor—in his underwear! The crowd gasped.

There was someone else on the stand now—someone tall, dark, and dressed in the sultan's robes. He held a snake staff in his right hand.

"Jafar!" Aladdin exclaimed.

Jafar turned with a sneer. *"Sultan* Jafar to you!"

"What manner of trickery is this!" the sultan demanded.

"Finders keepers," Jafar said. "I have the ultimate power now!"

A shadow fell over the courtyard. Everyone looked up.

Aladdin's breath caught in his throat. Abu and the carpet clutched each other in terror. Looming over them like an evil giant was the genie. He placed his hands on the palace as if he were about to crush it.

"Genie, stop!" Aladdin shouted. "What are you doing!"

The genie's eyes were full of sadness. "Sorry, kid," he said. "I've got a new master now."

With a mighty heave, he lifted the entire palace off

the ground. The people of Agrabah scattered, screaming as debris fell around them. The genie then flew to a mountain high above the city and set the palace down there.

Jafar let out a deep, triumphant laugh. "Now, you miserable wretches—bow to me!"

"We will *never* bow to you!" Jasmine replied. Aladdin and the sultan stood by her.

"Then you will cower!" Jafar said. He whirled around to face the genie. "My second wish is to be the most powerful sorcerer in the world!"

His snake staff began to glow, and green lightning crackled around it. Rajah let out a roar and lunged at Jafar. Jafar waved his staff, and in midair, Rajah was transformed into a kitten. As Rajah landed softly on his paws, Jafar glared at Jasmine and Aladdin. "Take a look at your precious Prince Ali—or should we say, *Aladdin!*"

A bolt of light shot from the staff. It surrounded Aladdin and Abu. Instantly Abu became a monkey again. Aladdin's robe, slippers, and turban disappeared. He fell to the floor, dressed in his old rags. "He's nothing more than a worthless lying street rat!"

Jasmine looked at him, confused and hurt. "Ali?"

"Jasmine . . . I'm sorry," Aladdin said.

"Face it, boy, you don't belong here," Jafar said.

"Uh, where does he belong? Could it be . . . the ends of the earth!" Iago taunted.

"Works for me!" Jafar cried as he waved his staff again.

Aladdin and Abu suddenly levitated off the ground and into the open window of a narrow tower. In an instant, the tower rocketed over the horizon. The carpet sped after it.

Jasmine watched in horror as the tower vanished over the horizon. The genie sadly turned away.

With a devious laugh, Jafar shouted, "At last! Agrabah is mine!"

CHAPTER THIRTEEN

W hen Aladdin awoke, he was cold—freezing cold. As he made his way out of a snowbank, an icy wind whipped snow into his face.

Where was he? Through the raging blizzard, he could see the tower lying in pieces, half-covered with snow. Just beyond it, a cliff plunged downward into darkness.

A crash . . . that was all he remembered. He must have been thrown out of the tower, unconscious.

A brown lump caught his attention. "Abu!" he called through chattering teeth. He raced over and dug his pet out of the snow. "Are you all right?"

Shivering, Abu nodded weakly.

Aladdin tucked Abu into his vest. "Oh, Abu, this is all my fault. I should have freed the genie when I had the chance. Somehow, I've got to go back and set things straight."

He felt a tickling sensation on his leg. Spinning

around, he saw the carpet reaching toward him. It was caught beneath a huge chunk of the tower.

Aladdin tried to pull the carpet free, but it was stuck tight. He and Abu started digging a trench around it, but the tower began to teeter.

"Look out!" Aladdin shouted. The tower began rolling toward them.

Calculating quickly, Aladdin ducked, curling Abu into his arms. The tower rolled over them, right where there was a window opening. Unharmed, they watched as the tower plunged over the cliff.

Freed from the tower, the carpet scooped up Aladdin and Abu and flew above the clouds.

"All right," cried Aladdin. "Now, back to Agrabah!"

Jafar loved the view from his new throne room. The palace was where it *belonged* now—on a mountaintop, not in the midst of the rabble. He happily sipped from his wine glass while the genie massaged his feet. The *former* sultan was now suspended from the ceiling like a marionette. He was dressed in a jester's outfit, and Jafar and Iago snickered at the ridiculous sight. Rajah, still a kitten, paced anxiously in a cage.

Jasmine sat at the window, her wrists in shackles, her eyes filled with sadness.

Jafar reached out with his staff. He hooked her shackles and pulled her close. "It pains me to see you reduced to this, Jasmine. You should be on the arm of the most powerful man in the world." With a wave of his staff, he made her chains vanish. A crown appeared on her head. "Why, with you as my queen—"

Jasmine took his glass and threw the wine in his face. "Never!"

Jafar bolted up from the throne. "Temper, temper, Jasmine," scolded Jafar. "You know what happens when you misbehave. . . . I'll teach you some respect!" He glared at the genie. "Genie, I have decided to make my final wish—I wish for Princess Jasmine to fall desperately in love with me!"

"No!" Jasmine said, backing away.

"Uh, Master," the genie said, "I can't do that—"

"You will do what I order you to do, slave!" Jafar roared as he grabbed the genie's beard.

Nobody noticed Aladdin and Abu peeking into the throne room window behind them—nobody except Jasmine.

She was about to scream when Aladdin shushed her

with a finger over his mouth. He, Abu, and the carpet climbed silently into the room.

Jasmine thought fast. "Jafar," she said with a seductive smile, "I never realized how incredibly handsome you are!"

Jafar spun around. His jaw hung open in disbelief— and so did the genie's.

"That's better," Jafar said. He slinked toward Jasmine, a cocky smile on his face. "Now, tell me more about . . . *myself.*"

"You're tall, dark . . ." Jasmine could see Aladdin, Abu, and the carpet sneaking toward the lamp. Now the genie saw them, too. He was trying to stifle an excited giggle.

"Go on . . . ," Jafar said.

Abu was inches from Iago now—and Iago was turning around. Jasmine quickly put her arms around Jafar, locking him in place. "You're well dressed," she continued. "You've stolen my heart. . . ."

With a quick leap, Abu grabbed Iago off his perch and put a hand over his mouth. They both tumbled to the ground.

"And the street rat!" Jafar said, drawing closer to Jasmine.

"*What* street rat?" Jasmine asked.

Crasssshhh! Abu and Iago knocked into a table, sending a pot to the ground.

Jafar started to turn. Jasmine had no choice but to pull him close and kiss him—passionately and on the lips.

Now was Aladdin's chance for action. But he couldn't move. All he could do was stare. There she was, the girl for whom he had risked his life, kissing . . . *him.*

Jafar pulled back. He was dazed with joy—until he saw the reflection of Aladdin in Jasmine's crown.

"You!" he said, whirling around in blind rage. His arm snapped forward, pointing his staff at Aladdin.

Zzzzzzap! A flash of light struck Aladdin in the chest. He flew backward, crashing into a pile of jewels.

"How many times do I have to kill you, boy?" Jafar said, drawing his arm back for a second shot.

Jamsine leapt at him, pushing his arm aside.

"You deceiving shrew!" Jafar snarled. "Your time is up!"

He turned his staff on Jasmine. Instantly she was trapped inside a giant hourglass. The upper chamber was full of sand, and it slowly spilled through the opening onto her. There was more than enough to bury her alive.

Zzzzzap! With a stroke of the staff, Jafar turned Abu into a cymbal-clanking toy monkey.

Zzzzzap! The carpet began to unravel. Aladdin ran to stop it. Jafar called out, "Things are unraveling fast, boy."

"This is all your fault, street rat! You never should have come back!" *Zzzzzzap!* Aladdin jumped back. A sword clattered to the ground beside him, then another. He looked up. Dozens of razor-sharp swords fell from the ceiling.

Jafar gestured again, and a wall of fire burst from the floor.

Aladdin grabbed one of the fallen swords. "Are you afraid to fight me yourself, you cowardly snake?" Aladdin said, batting away the swords as they fell.

Jafar made his way toward Aladdin, forcing him closer to the fire.

"A snake, am I? Perhaps you'd like to see how snakelike I can be!"

Jafar held out his snake staff with both hands. It began to grow, coming to hideous life, wrapping Jafar himself into its skin. Swelling, hissing, Jafar became a monstrous cobra, his head rising toward the ceiling. The flames rose with him, becoming a ring of deadly coils surrounding Aladdin.

With an unearthly roar, Jafar lunged. Aladdin swung his sword.

Shink! He struck two of Jafar's fangs, which clattered onto the floor.

"Rickum-rackum, stick that sword into that snake," the genie shouted.

"You stay out of this!" Jafar hissed. He lunged again, knocking Aladdin to the floor. The sword flew out of his hand.

"Ali!" the sultan cried, watching helplessly from above. "Jasmine!"

Aladdin rolled away, catching a glimpse of the hourglass. The sand had risen swiftly, covering all but Jasmine's head.

Without his sword, there was only one chance. Aladdin ran for the window and leapt onto the balcony. Jafar slithered after him. Quickly Aladdin ran back in, then ducked out another window.

Jafar followed from window to window, tangling his long body into a knot. He shrieked with pain.

Aladdin picked up his sword and ran toward the hourglass. Jasmine's nose was barely above the sand, her eyes wide with fear. Aladdin drew back the sword, ready to smash the glass.

With a resounding boom, Jafar pulled down the wall. He was free—and he threw his coils around Aladdin.

Aladdin's sword was caught in midair. He struggled to get loose. "You thought you could outwit the most powerful being on earth?" Jafar bellowed.

Aladdin wrenched left and right. In a corner of the room, the genie watched helplessly.

The genie!

Thinking fast, Aladdin said, "You're not so powerful. The genie has more power than you'll ever have! He gave you your power, and he can take it away!"

The genie ducked behind a pillar. "Al, what are you doing? Why are you bringing me into this?"

"Face it, Jafar, you're still just second," Aladdin continued.

Jafar loosened his coils. He turned his slimy face to the genie. "You're right. His power does exceed my own—but not for long!"

Aladdin fell to the floor as Jafar slithered across the

room. "Slave!" Jafar called to the genie. "I'm ready to make my third wish. I wish to be—an all-powerful genie!"

The genie looked at Aladdin, his blue face now chalk white. "Your wish," he said in a small, wavering voice, "is my command!"

CHAPTER FOURTEEN

*T*he genie gestured. A swirling current of energy encircled Jafar, and he began to change shape. The fire disappeared. His cobra body became wider and wider until he took on the roundness of a genie. "Yes!" Jafar shrieked. "The power! The absolute power!"

Quickly Aladdin picked up his sword and smashed the hourglass. Jasmine slid forward with the cascading sand. "What have you done!" she asked as Aladdin pulled her free.

Aladdin smiled. "Trust me."

"The universe is an open book before me!" Jafar yelled. "Mine to command, to control!" The dome of the palace exploded as Jafar rose to the sky.

Before he could say another word, gold shackles clamped around his wrists—just like the ones the genie wore. A lamp began to materialize beneath him, new and shiny.

"*Whaaat!* What is happening!" Jafar demanded.

"You wanted to be a genie!" Aladdin picked up the new lamp and held it out to Jafar. "You got it—and everything that goes with it!"

Jafar's legs were now a trail of vapor, a trail that disappeared into the lamp's spout. "No!" he said, his eyes bugging out in terror. "*Nooooooo!*"

Screaming with anguish, Jafar reached his hand upward. His fingers clasped Iago's feet. "Wha—hey! Let go!" Iago screamed.

With a dull *thoomp*, Jafar and Iago were sucked into the lamp.

Everyone in the throne room fell into an awed silence. Jasmine, the sultan, and the genie stared at Aladdin.

"Phenomenal cosmic powers," Aladdin said with a shrug. "Itty-bitty living space!"

The genie let out a loud cackle. "Al, you little genius!"

Instantly the room began to return to normal. Back on his feet, the sultan sighed with pleasure as his robes materialized on him. Abu became a live monkey again. Rajah grew back into a tiger, breaking free of his small cage. And the carpet looked brand new.

The genie grabbed the lamp and went to the balcony.

"Shall we? Ten thousand years in the Cave of Wonders ought to chill him out!" He wound up and hurled the lamp, sending it end over end toward the desert.

Smiling proudly, the genie flew outside. He grew to a gigantic shape, picked up the entire palace, and began carrying it back to its rightful place.

CHAPTER FIFTEEN

*L*ater that day, when Agrabah had returned to normal, Jasmine and Aladdin stood on the throne room balcony.

"Jasmine," Aladdin said softly, "I'm sorry I lied to you . . . about being a prince."

Jasmine nodded. "I know why you did."

"I guess . . . this is good-bye!"

Jasmine turned away. "That stupid law! It isn't fair!" Slowly, tearfully, she faced Aladdin again. "I love you."

Suddenly the genie popped through the window. "Al, no problem—you've got one wish left. Just say the word, and you're a prince again!"

"But Genie," Aladdin said. "What about your freedom!"

"Al, you're in love. You're not going to find another girl like this in a million years. Believe me, I've looked."

Aladdin looked from the genie to Jasmine. He knew how much freedom meant now. Not only to the genie but to Jasmine—and to himself. Just as she needed to be free of the sultan's laws, Aladdin needed to be free, too. Free to be himself.

"Jasmine . . . I do love you," he finally said. "But I can't pretend to be something I'm not."

Jasmine bowed her head. "I understand."

"Genie," Aladdin said, "I wish for your freedom. It's about time I started keeping my promises."

In a flash, the genie's gold cuffs vanished. He was stunned. "Quick! Wish for something—anything! Say, 'I want the Nile!' "

"Er—I wish for the Nile," Aladdin said.

"NO WAY!" said the genie, with a laugh. "I'm free!" he shouted, his face lighting up. "I'm free! I'm off to see the world!"

"Congratulations!" the sultan said, peeking out behind him.

"Genie, I'm going to miss you," Aladdin said.

"Me, too, Al," the genie replied with a fond smile. "No matter what anybody says, you'll always be a prince to me!"

"That's right!" the sultan agreed. "You've certainly proved your worth as far as I'm concerned. If it's the law that's the problem, then what we need is a new law!"

Jasmine looked at him, stunned. "Father?"

"From this day forth, the princess shall marry whomever she deems worthy!"

"I choose you, Aladdin!" Jasmine cried instantly.

Aladdin was ecstatic. "Call me Al," he said.

He and Jasmine burst out laughing. Aladdin took her in his arms, and the two of them began twirling around the balcony.

"Well!" the genie said with a huge smile. "I can't do any more damage around here. And now I am out of here! Bye-bye, you crazy lovebirds!"

Like a rocket, the genie launched himself into the sky. The sultan followed him with his eyes until the genie disappeared over the horizon.

Aladdin and Jasmine didn't even notice him leave. As they shared a long, dreamy kiss, they didn't notice much of anything—except each other.